Bad News

Shoes

Written by Dixie B. Gaisford

Illustrated by Suzanne Smith

My shoes are tight.

I need some more.

Mama and I head for the store.

I spy a pair.

"Oh, buy me these!"

Instead my mama only sees . . .

. . . Ugly shoes,

Brown shoes,

Thudding-up-and-down shoes,

Clunky shoes,

Strangly shoes,

Laces-long-and-tangly shoes, . . .

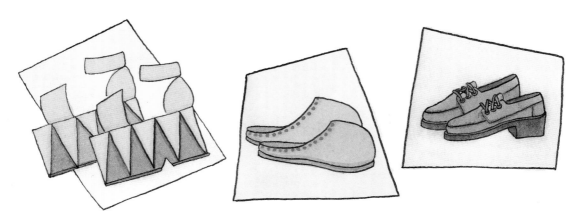

Thick-soled shoes,

Stout shoes,

Never-wear-them-out shoes,

Boring shoes,

Sport shoes,

These-have-good-support shoes, . . .

. . . Stomper shoes,

Lumpy shoes,

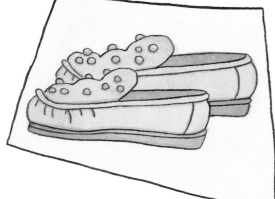

Frumpy, dumpy, grumpy shoes!

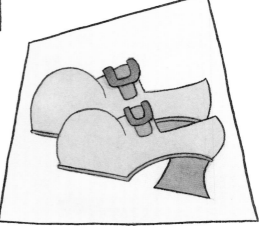

I want to say
I will refuse
To wear them if I cannot choose . . .

. . . Sleek shoes,

Slip-on shoes,

Peppy off-and-on shoes,

Pointy shoes,

Dazzling shoes,

Fancy razzmatazzling shoes, . . .

Thin-strap shoes,

Flower shoes,

Dancing-by-the-hour shoes,

Velvet shoes,

Bow shoes,

Princess-long-ago shoes, . . .

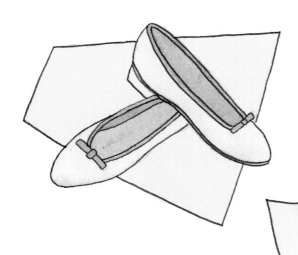

. . . Dainty shoes,

Sweet shoes,

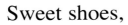

Light-upon-my-feet shoes!

I pout, I moan.

I act confused.

But Mama's not a bit amused.

She snaps her purse.

Looks like I lose

'Cause Mama buys those bad-news shoes.